Keith Canedo was born in Los Angeles, California, and is a member of the Society of Children's Book Writers and Illustrators. He is a children's picture book author, cartoonist, musician, and writer of historical fiction novels.
He currently lives in Seattle, Washington.

Adriane Hairston was born in Pittsburgh, Pennsylvania, and is an award-winning artist-illustrator formally trained at the Tyler School of Art at Temple University with numerous exhibitions and collaborations.
She currently lives in Cle Elum, Washington.

AUSTIN MACAULEY PUBLISHERS™
LONDON • CAMBRIDGE • NEW YORK • SHARJAH

Have You Seen Green?

Keith Canedo
Illustrated by Adriane Hairston

Copyright © Keith Canedo (2020)

Ordering Information
Quantity sales: Special discounts are available on quantity purchases by corporations, associations, and others. For details, contact the publisher at the address below.

Publisher's Cataloging-in-Publication data
Canedo, Keith
Have You Seen Green?

ISBN 9781647506674 (Paperback)
ISBN 9781647506667 (Hardback)
ISBN 9781647506681 (ePub e-book)

Library of Congress Control Number: 2020913676

www.austinmacauley.com/us

First Published (2020)
Austin Macauley Publishers LLC
40 Wall Street, 28th Floor
New York, NY 10005
USA

mail-usa@austinmacauley.com
+1 (646) 5125767

For Micaela, Kelsey, Jacob, Dominic, and Claire – the best kids I know.
And the children and caregivers at the Ronald McDonald House.

Keith

To my beloved supporters, thank you for never giving up on me. To Earth,
thank you for all your nourishment, we won't give up on you.

Adriane

Rain, rain, like needles and pins.
But after it stops the magic begins.

The great rainbow spirits danced high above.
Spreading their joy and sending their love.

Jacob looked up and wondered why
the green spirit was missing and not in the sky.

The spirits asked Jacob, "please find our green
so our full rainbow family will always be seen."

Jacob went to the frog in the pond and asked,
"have you seen green?"

"I'm sorry to say it's been fading away,
ask the forest of trees what they've seen."

Jacob went to the forest of trees and asked,
"have you seen green?"

"We're sorry to say it's been fading away,
ask the grass in the park what they've seen."

Jacob went to the grass in the park and asked, "have you seen green?"

"We're sorry to say it's been fading away,
ask the fish in the sea what he's seen."

Jacob went to the fish in the sea and asked,
"have you seen green?"

" I'm sorry to say it's been fading away,
ask the people in town what they've seen."

But factories and cars and trips
to the stars took up all of their valuable time.

"It's not our affair so we just don't care why
the color green doesn't shine."

A sad little Jacob walked alone on the shore.
"Doesn't anyone care about green anymore?"

"I do," said a small voice that was almost not heard.
Washed up on the beach was an oil-covered bird.

The little bird told him, "you've already seen green.
You just don't remember when they were clean."

Jacob thought of the frog in the pond and the forest of trees, the grass in the park and the fish in the sea.

"Their green colors fade when we don't try,
to take care of our lands and oceans and sky."

"But I'm only one kid, what can I do?"
"Change starts with just one, let it be you".

Then the bird jumped up and started to fly.
And smiled back at Jacob with the wink of an eye.

At last Jacob knew where to find green.
He simply needed to keep the earth clean.

Friends at school began to help out,
working together would bring change about.

They started recycling and turning off lights.
Picking up litter, hauling leaves on their bikes.

Sweeping the rivers and unclogging streams,
doing what's needed to bring back the green.

Help started coming from kids everywhere,
to clean up the planet that they all share.

When they all worked together and volunteered,
slowly the color of green reappeared.

The grateful spirits were a family once more.
Their rainbow was perfect just like before.

Soon a blanket of green was gently unfurled
on the trees parks and forests all over the world.

And if green in the rainbows was starting to fade,
the children remembered the promise they made.

To the oil-covered bird wherever she flies,
to honor the lands and oceans and skies.

CPSIA information can be obtained
at www.ICGtesting.com
Printed in the USA
LVHW021928181220
674522LV00009B/655

9 781647 506674